THE BOYS THAT ALMOST MADE IT

Britt Gilmore

Author's Tranquility Press
MARIETTA, GEORGIA

Copyright © 2022 by Britt Gilmore.

All rights reserved. No part of this publication may be reproduced, distributed, or transmitted in any form or by any means, including photocopying, recording, or other electronic or mechanical methods, without the prior written permission of the publisher, except in the case of brief quotations embodied in critical reviews and certain other noncommercial uses permitted by copyright law. For permission requests, write to the publisher, addressed "Attention: Permissions Coordinator," at the address below.

Britt Gilmore /Author's Tranquility Press
2706 Station Club Drive SW
Marietta, GA 30060
www.authorstranquilitypress.com

Ordering Information:
Quantity sales. Special discounts are available on quantity purchases by corporations, associations, and others. For details, contact the "Special Sales Department" at the address above.

The Boys That Almost Made It/ Britt Gilmore
Paperback 978-1-959453-40-6
Ebook 978-1-959453-41-3

THE BOYS THAT ALMOST MADE IT

Britt Gilmore

Here's my story of three brothers that came close to achieving their dream in the music business.

Britt, Terry (Big T), and Bo Gilmore are these brothers, "The Rangers."

It starts with our father's dream of having 3 sons so he could have his own "home-grown quartet." Our father, Charlie Gilmore (Big C), was one of the best Bass singers (in my opinion, the best) that ever sang a low note! Check him out on YouTube; "Walk That Lonesome Road" by The Rangers/Gilmore Brothers.

Our Dad achieved his dream; he did have three sons who were one of the best Southern Gospel Quartets/Country Groups that ever graced the stage.

Let's start with some history of who the Gilmores are and where they come from...

The year is the early 1940s; it's about an hour before daybreak, and the Gilmore household is already busy. The meat wasn't from the store; it came from the smokehouse, the eggs weren't from the store, they came from the hen house, and the grits and coffee were store-bought! The smell of sausage, bacon, grits, eggs and coffee filled the house on that cold morning in rural Alabama, fixing to be demolished by a hungry crew of 13!

Daddy Harve and Mama Coy (my grandparents on my Dad's side), Sara, Ruby, Warren, Charlie, Dorothy, Bryan, Earl, Martha, Johnny, Mary, and Maxine; this is my Dad's family. After breakfast, Uncle Warren, my Dad, Uncle Brian, Uncle Johnny, and Uncle Earl go outside and hitch up the mules to the wagon. Mama Coy and the girls are busy doing their daily chores. Once everything is loaded in the wagon, including all the boys and Daddy Harve, they head to the fields where they will be until the sun is setting low in the west. It was tough back then, but they didn't complain or even act like they knew how tough it was. Every Sunday morning that same wagon and mule would take my rather large family to our home church (Sardis Freewill Baptist) located deep in the woods, heck everything back then was in the woods!

Here's a story my Dad told; he was in the corn field picking corn, but he had himself a cornstalk and pretended it was his microphone which he had heard about from listening to the Grand Ole Opry on Saturday night on the radio, he didn't know what a microphone looked like, so he assumed the cornstalk would have to do. He started singing into that cornstalk instead of picking corn. My grandfather (Daddy Harve) caught him doing that and wore him out for not picking corn!

Our Dad loved music from an early age. He told us he would walk miles to singing schools which were quite popular back in those days down in the south. He and his brothers formed a quartet they called themselves, The Gilmore Brothers. They were a four-part harmony southern gospel quartet. They were very good but never were able to keep it together in order to do anything with it because they all got married. They had to work jobs that didn't allow them the time to do their music.

Sardis Freewill Baptist church was the home church of almost everyone within 20 country miles! Once the piano player rolled out the first intro to the old gospel hymns and everyone started singing, you knew you were in for a great service! The fiery little red-faced preacher hit the pulpit, slamming his fist down on it, yelling at the top of his lungs! He warned of fire and brimstone and just how hot hell would be if you didn't straighten up your sorry wicked ways! After church, there was always a feast at our Grandparent's house, heck it was like Thanksgiving every Sunday at the Gilmore house!

Picture this; it's Sunday afternoon at the Gilmore's farm; there is Daddy Harve and Mama Coy; Uncle Warren and Aunt Peggy with their kids, Stevie, Karen, Ginger, and Johna; Aunt Sara and Uncle Roy with their kids, Tommy, Mike, Candy, Dianna and Lisa; Charlie (our Dad) and my mom Linda and their kids, Terry (Big T), Britt (that's me) Bo, Kathy and Tammy; Aunt Ruby and Uncle Becker their kids, Billy and Debra; Aunt Dot and Uncle Tom, their kids Wayne, Junior and Evelyn; Uncle Brian and Aunt Julene and their kids Patty, Tracy and Jennings; Aunt Mot and Uncle RL and their kids, Skeet, Carla and Mike; Uncle Earl and Aunt Jean and their kids, Kim, Kelly and Frannie; Uncle Johnny and Aunt Georgia Faye and their kids Bill, Melissa, Ricky, Mickey and John; Aunt Mary and Uncle Billy and their kids, Carmen, Mary Helen and Sheila; Aunt Maxine and Uncle Bobby and their kids Jackie and Robin.

Folks, that's a big crew of people to feed! There were 62 of us when we were all there, which was every Sunday. We always had friends there as well, sometimes, the preacher and his family would join us. Mama Coy assigned each daughter and daughter-in-law with what they were to bring to the feast!

All of us cousin's played games that I'm quite sure the young people of today have never heard of. For example, there were these tall sticky weeds called dog fennels, we would all get us about 4 or 5 dog fennels, bundle them up and tie them together in a club-like shape. We would then go out to the barn and stir up the wasp nests that were sure to be there. As the wasps were attacking us like jet fighter planes, we would swat them out of the air with our dog fennels! We didn't always win! I have seen many swollen eyes and fat lips made by those fiery little wasps that got through our defenses!

We had a huge field that wasn't exactly flat, but it served well enough to be our football field. We played every Sunday afternoon, we played really hard! We didn't have helmets, pads, mouthpieces, folks this wasn't flag or touch football, this was laying one of your cousins out! This was football with a violent hit like you might see on TV! Just like our Grandad and Dad's, we were all tough as lighter stumps, we feared nothing or no one but God!

One of those Sundays, I was 5 years old. I had on a pair of cowboy boots. I got into the hog pen, my boots got stuck in the mud; I just came out of them and kept getting up barefooted! Aunt Mot looked out from the porch just after I got out of sight; saw just my little boots stuck in the mud and started freaking out and screaming. Everyone ran outside trying to see what was wrong, she was screaming the hogs had eaten me! I am sure my precious little mom had a very touchy moment before everyone figured out, I wasn't eaten, I was just fine.

There are so many stories throughout my childhood, these are wonderful stories told by all the family members I have mentioned. The best storyteller out of the Gilmore bunch was Uncle Earl! This man is as funny as any comedian who ever lived. I don't say that because he's my uncle, I know talent, Uncle Earl is very talented! He told stories that were so funny; he would have you bent over with your sides hurting from laughing so hard. These were very hard and tough people, heck they had to be, to survive!

Uncle Warren, we called him Dead-Eye because if his gun went up and fired you could go get the meat, he was a deadly shot, therefore earning his nickname! Dead-Eye, who, by the way (don't tell anyone) was my favorite! He was the toughest man I have ever known. There are many great and very funny stories I could share with you about Dead-Eye, he was something special for sure.

The Gilmores were very proud, God-fearing people. The men were tough and handsome, the ladies were beautiful and sweet. This tradition continued up until Daddy Harve had a massive heart attack. He and my cousin Stevie (Lightning) were trying to put a yoke on a bull's neck so the bull couldn't break through the fence. Daddy Harve told Lightning to hold the bull, he would be back soon; but Daddy Harve never came back. We got the call at our house as we were eating supper; my Dad answered the phone, he listened to whoever was on the other end, one of my aunts or uncles the best I remember. My Dad hung up the phone, never said a word and walked out of the room. We all got up to see what was wrong. In my 13 years on earth, I had never seen my tough ole Daddy cry, I did that night. This was a sad time for the Gilmore family, our patriarch was gone.

A couple of days before Daddy Harve died, we had put the finishing touches on a song; we picked up the phone and sang our song to Daddy Harve.

"What a Day" was the name of the song; it is still one of my favorite songs. I couldn't swear to it but I believe Daddy Harve must have had a tear in his eye because that song was one of his favorites, it was beautiful.

Daddy Harve never heard us sing again, he passed away two days later. The old folks say my Granddad was a great singer as well; I never heard him sing; when I was very young, he got throat cancer, had an operation in Birmingham, AL, and talked in a whisper for the rest of his life. They say he could blow the rafters off the church with his big booming voice!

Mama Coy was beautiful, she could sing like an angel they say. She would have people coming from all over the county to hear her sing; from what I'm told the boys came to see her beauty, that was before Daddy Harve swept her off of her feet!

I miss those days; I miss the closeness we had as a huge, happy, proud family. I can honestly say there isn't a family in the world better than the Gilmore family, might be some just as good, but none better! Looking back on it now, Daddy Harve was the glue that held the Gilmore family together. He was a very tough man, one who didn't take any junk and didn't give any junk. He was as tough as any man alive, strong too! He didn't care how big you were; he loved to wrestle, he would throw you to the ground before you knew it and have you pinned down! There are so many wonderful memories of my Gilmore Family which I will cherish until the day I ride my last trail.

My mom's side of the family were wonderful people as well, Mama Ree and Paw (my grandmother and grandfather on her side). My grandfather (Paw) taught us a lot about the outdoors; farming, hunting, and fishing, he was an awesome man! Mama Ree was probably the best cook that ever lived, next to my mom! We had an uncle named Mantz Hatfield that could do anything with a whole lot of nothing, I truly believe uncle Mantz was a genius! We spent a lot of time growing up at our grandparents' house, heck we never wanted to leave!

There you go, a little background on where The Rangers/Gilmore Brothers came from.

Let's switch gears, come take a ride with me down the road we traveled, you will see why I titled this book "The Boys That Almost Made It."

Big C sang bass, my brother Big T sang tenor, my brother Bo sang lead/baritone, and I sang baritone/lead. My uncle, Jerry Redd played the piano and sang as well. Jerry Redd was one of the most talented men I have ever known. Folks, there was something magical when we put those parts together, some of the prettiest and tightest harmonies ever sang.

Ok boys, let's go rehearse, Big C says. After spending an hour or so rehearsing the songs without instruments (acapella); here we go, off to Sardis Free Will Baptist Church, located between Clayton and Eufaula, AL. We would practice at that little country church for many hours. Big C would pop us well if we sang off the pitch (sharp or flat). Bo and me hardly ever sang off pitch, but my poor brother Big T caught hell! Big T loved singing as much as my Dad did; he liked to be clean, looking slick all the time. Bo and I were totally the other way; when we were young, we could care less and hated dressing up or taking a bath!

One day we were playing football in a field across the road from where we lived, my Dad and Big T pulls up; my Dad called me over "get in the car son, we have to sing tonight". I was filthy; I was hot, both mentally and physically. Here I am, in a very important football game, now I had to put on that stupid-looking little double-breasted blue blazer; all the while I have sweat beads under my neck and arms, man was I pissed off! I'm quite sure I smelled something like a goat as well! Well, I kept all of this to myself because my Dad DID NOT TOLERATE any back talk. I got my filthy little rump in the backseat and went and sang for Jesus or may I say on this particular night, for my Dad! Jesus knows what we are thinking; I doubt I was free of good thinking on that night!

Ok boys, we are going to cut an album, Big C says. I am excited, I'm eleven years old and going to cut our 1st album, but I'm somewhat sad; I have to miss another one of my football games to go do what my Dad and Big T loved more than anything, singing!

My Dad, Big T, Bo and me hit the road to Bainbridge, GA. We drive about two hours to a studio a friend of my Dad owns in Bainbridge, GA; his name was Jack Martin. Jack was the bass singer for a group called The Sunshine Boys, also there was Ace Richmond, who also sang with the Sunshine Boys. My Dad, Big T and I were doing the singing (Bo was too young), Ace Richmond played bass guitar, Jimmy Potter played the snare drum and Lamond Cloud played the piano, Mr. Jack was the engineer.

We were called the Lakesmen's back then; I suppose that was because we grew up on Lake Eufaula. I really don't remember how long it took, although I thought I would never get back home! We had our 1st album cut! About two months later, we got 500 copies of that album and started selling them when we would go to sing at a church, ballfield, auditorium or anywhere else Dad booked us to sing. We were poor and could not afford an album cover, so we just had those white sleeves that the album came in back then! After we came off stage my brothers and I would go out through the audience with an arm full of albums selling those things like crazy! Looking back on it, I'm sure some of those people bought those albums because they felt sorry for us! Don't get me wrong, we were always a good group; we could hold our own with any of the well-known professional groups.

A little short history on Southern Gospel, I have been associated with Southern Gospel, Country, Southern Rock and Motown, but the ole boys from the Southern Gospel era would have made those other guys blush! I don't know what it was about 5 guys, all dressed in matching suits, singing; let's just say if it was good, it was magical!

We were at our home church having an all-day singing and dinner on the ground, which in the south back in that time was very popular. It's 1968; ABC, CBS or NBC is there with big cameras everywhere, they are filming a national TV special for a candidate who was running for President of the United States of America, his name was George C Wallace who happened to be friends with my Dad. George, was from our home county; Barbour County, Alabama. George was the Governor of Alabama. My first name is Wallace, yep you guessed right, my Dad named me after George C. Wallace back in 1955 when George was our Circuit Judge. Even though George stood on the steps at the University of Alabama to block segregation, he later got more votes in Alabama than any person in history and a large part of that vote was the black vote. I don't know why we all just can't get along and love one another...?

Here is a piece I wrote on racism a while back; I hope it hits home and you can take something from it, if it speaks to you...

Racism Comes from the Heart "*Of Each Individual*"

Hello, I am Britt Gilmore; I was born in rural Alabama in 1955; I was named after George C. Wallace, my full name is Wallace Britt Gilmore. George Wallace was the circuit judge and later Governor of Alabama; he ran for President in 1968, he was leading in the polls before he was shot and severely wounded in Maryland while on the campaign trail.

My Dad (Charlie Gilmore) was county sheriff in Barbour County Alabama. My Dad hired the first black deputy in the state of Alabama, his name was Jack Knight, Jack was awesome! He was a great friend of ours, we would often go raccoon hunting at night with Jack. Jack had a son named Tyrone, Tyrone is the first person I had ever heard do rap, he was definitely before his time!

As history shows, those were definitely trying times when it came to race relations. Our Dad and Mom taught us that all people were equal in the eyes of God. I am thankful for the way we were raised; but I grew up around some that viewed things quite differently. I tell you that to say this; regardless of your background or upbringing, you are what you allow yourself to be. I have witnessed racism throughout my life, both from blacks and whites. I never understood why some people were this way, heck there isn't but one race! Regardless of what color you are, you're part of *"THE HUMAN RACE"*.

Racism will always be here, for we are always going to have people with hatred in their hearts. Racism is bad, it doesn't matter what color you are. These politicians that stir things up using the race card are just as bad or worse as the person calling someone a bad word. Have you ever noticed that when everything else fell, the politicians bring up the race card!

I don't understand why black people support the Democrats, heck they were/are the KKK, they killed Martin Luther King Jr, they were Jim Crow, and you had a sitting President make a statement; "I'll have the black "he used the N word though" people voting for Democrats for the next 100 years! That was Democratic President Lyndon B. Johnson.

God sees all of us as his creation. Do you think God approves of what these people do or think…? I surely don't. Here's what each person must do to erase the racist feelings towards another human being; realize that we are all God's children; God's opinion is definitely the "only one that matters."

Here's some great advice (Many receive advice, but only the wise profit from it), get on your knees and ask God for the forgiveness of your racial hatred. It all starts with (YOU) each individual, regardless of your skin color. For in the end, what is in each of our hearts will be all that matters, you will not fool God.

We can all help cure racism by first making sure each of our hearts is pure and we are not influenced by those that aren't. Be your own person, use your own brain, and cleanse your heart of hatred and racism…

Kindly,

Britt Gilmore

We also went every year to Red Level, Alabama to perform at the "Hank Williams Memorial Day" event. Hank Jr. was always there as well. Looking back on everything, I would not take anything for the way we were raised, we had awesome parents. Young people today don't really understand the way it was back then, it is totally different these days. I am sad because my son will never experience some of the things I experienced, but on the other hand, I'm glad he won't experience some of what I have.

Getting back to my Dad, he was without a doubt the best bass singer that ever lived; some say JD Sumner was, but JD himself said he had never heard a voice like Charlie Gilmore's. JD tried to hire my Dad to sing with his group back in the 60s, The Stamps Quartet, which later backed up Elvis Presley. My Dad had other ideas with his boys and graciously declined. He and JD remained friends until death took them both away.

A few years go by; my Dad runs for sheriff in our home county and wins. That sort of backed the singing off a little, even though we would still do it at least 3 or 4 times a month. I am 15 at this time; I definitely have other things on my mind. In 1972 we go to Bristol, VA and record a new album in a real professional studio with real professional studio musicians. Oh, by the way, our name had been changed to The Rangers. The Rangers was a name that originated in Dallas, TX back in the 1930s by two brothers, Arnold and Vernon Hyles. One of the brothers was a friend of my Dad's. After they retired, they gave us the right to use the Ranger's name, so we became The Rangers. Hears a little story for you; The rock group "NIGHT RANGER" is called that because back in the early 80s, they were set to release their debut album as "The Rangers" until one of them saw our picture in Billboard magazine.

They told us they had to ditch a lot of promo materials because of that.

This album was awesome; it was Big T, Bo, Jerry Redd, my Dad and me. We had a piano player named Stan Turner who was one of our lifelong friends. Jerry Redd was one of the most musically talented men I have ever known. Jerry could play anything; he had a voice that was a special gift from God. Jerry sang with some of the most well-known southern gospel groups ever, The Stamps, The Kingsmen, The Plainsmen, The Diplomats and The Speer Family. Jerry taught my brothers and me how to sing, sing correctly that is. We could always sing, we all had the God-given talent, but singing and singing correctly are two different things.

After all, was done, we had an album that turned out to be really good so "Better than Ever", is what we called it! This album had a real album cover; it was really professional! It was called; The Rangers "Better than Ever". The Rangers had some awesome groups throughout the years. I'm not saying we were the best, but I am saying we were just as good as any of those before us.

Southern Gospel music was very big from the 1930s up until the 1980s. Not sure why, but it has taken a backseat in the world of music today. I hope it comes back around one of these days. It is 1973; it's time for my Dad to decide if he wants to run for sheriff again. I know what he most wanted; he would get his boys and hit the road singing full time! As I said earlier, we were not rich. My Dad and Mom had to do the things they had to do with 5 kids. When you have 5 children, you did what you had to do to raise them. Even though County Sheriff was a prestigious position to have in your county, the pay sure wasn't too good back then!

It is now 1975; my Dad runs again for sheriff and is reelected. The Rangers are still kicking it around and making a little noise in the business. The legendary Hovie Lister joins the group in 1975 and things are looking up! I don't just throw the term "Legendary" around loosely. Hovie was the King of southern gospel music and one of Elvis Presley's favorites. He had one of the best quartet's ever, "Hovie Lister and the Statesmen's Quartet." They were the first music groups of any kind to have their own syndicated TV show with major sponsors. We knew all the Statesmen; Doy Ott, Jim "Big Chief" Weatherington, Jake Hess and Denver Crumpler, Rosie Rosell, and Sherrill Nielson they were something to see when they took the stage! The Statesmen disbanded after the death of Big Chief and Hovie Lister joined our group The Rangers. We hit the road in a big way, we had a tour bus, and we had dates from coast to coast! The Ranger's reputation of being a very good Southern Gospel Quartet was growing!

It is 1975, we are headed out west, when we get to Memphis, Hovie tells our bus driver Earl Black (Blackie) to head to Elvis Presley Boulevard. At first, I thought he was joking. We pulled up to the gate of Graceland Hovie gets off the bus and hugs an older gentleman there at the gate, later on we found out that Virgil was Elvis Presley's, I couldn't believe it! We're going to meet Elvis!

We pull our bus up to Graceland; go into the front parlor just off to the right as you enter the front door of Graceland, waiting for Elvis. Elvis comes down his staircase with some Cepacol mouthwash, toothpaste and toothbrushes. Elvis starts throwing them to each of us and says, *"I don't sing with anyone who has stinking breath! He starts laughing like crazy"*! He was making a joke; they said he was quite the prankster.

We gathered around a piano and sang for many hours. Elvis was quite smitten with my Dad's bass voice; he loved good bass singers. Let me tell you, it was totally awesome! I'm 20 years old, in Hog Heaven, are you kidding me, this is Elvis Presley!

Elvis was very nice, he was great. It was like sitting, and talking with one of my brothers, what a gentleman he was. A little after daylight the next morning, we ate breakfast (with Elvis!) and left Graceland.

We leave on our westward trail; we head up through Oklahoma, Kansas, and Missouri. One night we are on the show with a group that is very hot at the time "Willie Wynn and The Tennesseans". I believe Hovie was ticked off because we were not closing the show. It was almost time for us to go on stage, Hovie wasn't even ready! He looked as though he hadn't combed his hair for a week, I was thinking, what's up with Hovie...?

Hovie gets us together and says; boys, I want all of you to put your best foot forward, let's leave this stage so hot that the guys trying to follow us will have a rough time doing it. Hovie puts his black pinstripe suit on and gets off the bus; I'm wondering, "what's he going to do about that hair...? Hovie walks over to a water spicket on the side of the auditorium, sticks his head under the water, pulls out his comb and slicks his hair back like a gangster! We hit that stage with a vengeance; I've never seen anyone as masterful as Hovie Lister that night; we brought the house down! We come off the stage, Willie and The Tennesseans are looking pretty shaken as we walk by, Hovie calmly says, follow that!

We left there and headed into Kansas. We had always looked up to Hovie, heck we put Hovie on a pedestal. Don't get me wrong, Hovie was a great man but he battled demons just like any other person might, no one is perfect. We finished that tour and had a lot of dates booked, but for a very personal reason to my family, we never filled them.

I look back now, and I know why, but it is not worth talking about. I could see my Dad had given up on his desire to be sheriff any longer. My Dad and mom get a divorce; my siblings and I are devastated! My brothers and I go our separate ways. My mom and sisters try and do the best they can after my Dad leaves. It was heartbreaking. I will never reveal the why or the who's, but it was not something I wanted to be around, let's just say some people's choices sucked!

I am at a crossroads; I quit singing, and I hit the road with a company called Pittsburg Des Moines Steel. We go all over the country building huge and sometimes very high tanks; these were gas tanks, water tanks, smokestacks, chemical tanks, etc.... I do this for a couple of years; I am in Lake Charles, Louisiana; my brother Big T calls me; Britt, I have us a deal in Nashville, TN. Man did that sound great to me! Ladies and Gentlemen, if you ever have the opportunity to build tanks, turn it down! That is by far the hardest work on this earth! You make great money, but I guarantee you, it isn't enough! I packed my bags and head to Nashville to be a star!

Big T, Bo and I start the journey of getting our act together and opening some doors and turning some heads. We sign a contract with an organization. Remember, we are just country boys from Alabama that knew the world was round, but just not how round! We put together a group of musicians for our band, got us a bus, got us bookings at nightclubs and started chiseling out our country music career!

The first nightclub we were booked into was for three nights, Thursday, Friday and Saturday in Decatur, Illinois at D'S Country Lounge. Our bus pulls out back of the place, we go inside and WOW! The stage is up behind the bar! You have to keep in mind; that we were used to playing in churches, auditoriums, ball fields, etc.... Boys there's the stage, we are singing up behind the bar! I was beginning to wonder if I should have stayed on that tank!

Let me lay this one out for you; before we hit the road; Big T had taken us down to a clothing store in Nashville on Broadway called The Alamo. It was the place where Grand Ole Opry stars bought their shiny rhinestone stage suits. We get suits made to match, they not only have rhinestones, but they have these flared leg pants (like Elvis wore) the flare was a different color than the pants color, a ruffled shirt, vest with rhinestones and white patented leather boots! We hit the stage singing Proud Mary in Decatur, Illinois, up behind the bar, looking good!

We were an instant hit at D'S Country Lounge! This is the first time we were bombarded by ladies looking for adventure; you wouldn't believe me if I told you, so I won't. We will keep this book G-rated so my grandkids can read it!

Word spread fast, by Saturday night, you could not get in the place, much less find a seat! We had club owners from other cities there as well, by the time we got back to Nashville our agent had The Rangers booked for six months straight, just in Illinois!

We had a lady from Nashville, Vernell Hackett doing publicity for us, Vernell was great! We are feeling pretty good about ourselves, we are making a living, singing!

We went to the studio for the first time as a country group. We cut songs our manager at the time picked for us. The musicians were awesome, Pig Robbins was playing the session, he was the biggest named studio piano player for years in Nashville, and another legend, Buddy Emmons, was playing the steel guitar. Fred Newell was playing lead guitar, another legend. The project was good, the singing was good, and the mix came out good, but it was not original material, without original material, you didn't get a record deal. One of the songs got the rumor mill in Nashville cranked up for the 1st time about the new group in town called The Rangers, the song was Mohair Sam; it was a great cut, heck I don't even have a copy of it anymore, wish I did!

We were doing a showcase at the Hilton Hotel in Nashville one night; a gentleman by the name of Mr. Harry "Hap" Peeples" came to see us. Mr. Peeples was one of the country's most successful concert promoters, especially west of the Mississippi. Country music legend Governor Jimmie Davis was Mr. Peeples's guest at our show that night, it was really cool getting to meet him. We put on a great show that night. Mr. Peeples asked us to meet with him.

We went and met with Mr. Peeples and his awesome assistant, Ms. Evelyn that next day. We agreed on a deal for The Rangers to work all his fairs/concerts/festivals, etc. which he represented all over the country. Our manager at the time wasn't interested in going to our showcase for Mr. Peeples or attending the meeting. Our short-term agreement with him was up, he was trying to get us to sign this long-term contract that best I remember, was not in our favor. I suppose he thought we were a bunch of country boys from Alabama that had come in on the truck that night, well, we came in on the truck alright, but we were driving it!

So, we met with him and let him know we would be taking a different direction and he wasn't in it! Don't worry, he didn't set up at the showcase with Mr. Peeples, Big T did that.

Mr. Peeples and Big T got us out of the nightclubs; we only played one more nightclub ever in our career after that: Billy Bob's in Ft Worth, TX., but that was like playing a concert hall.

The first place Mr. Peeples booked us was the Oklahoma State Fair; we did two shows a day, one in the afternoon and one at night. We had a great band; man, those boys were good! Our band consisted of piano, drums, lead guitar, rhythm guitar, bass guitar, steel guitar, fiddle and saxophone. We had a tight, high-energy show; Mr. Peeples started getting calls for The Rangers!

We left there; we went to the Texas State Fair in Dallas; we were to open for a group that had a hit song playing on the radio at the time. That was fine with us; we opened the show. We remembered what Hovie taught us, and we left that stage hotter than a $2 pistol!

The group's manager called Mr. Peeples the next day, he said we could not open for his group because we were just too dynamic. Mr. Peeples kindly told that group's manager, no problem, your act could open for The Rangers! Look, we never hit a stage with any kind of bad intent for another act; we hit the stage with one purpose, to entertain our audience the very best we could. Hey, if we left that stage hotter than a firecracker, so be it. As Hovie said, "follow that one boy's"!

We played the Texas State Fair in Dallas, TX for 10 days, two shows a day. We left there and went on a string of fairs all over the mid-west, life was good. A very good thing about playing these fairs was we got to hit the midway and ride all the rides we wanted to, free! That was part of our deal which Mr. Peeples negotiated for us, heck we didn't even know it!

Once the fair season was over in America, we would go into Canada and play. They paid really good money in the dead of winter in Canada and those Canadian girls were quite friendly, pretty too, they loved the way we talked!

One of our favorite places was in Calgary, Canada at a huge club called Danny Hoopers Stockyard, it was an old Methodist church that was absolutely beautiful. Our host, Danny Hooper was an entertainer/songwriter as well. About the 3rd time The Rangers played there, Danny told us he had written a song about us titled "Daddy, lock your daughters up; The Boys are Back in Town". Danny was always messing with us; I don't have a clue what gave him the idea for that one!

We went to Sadia Arabia for 3 weeks for Aramco Oil Company, that was quite an experience. Looking back on it now, it's a wonder we didn't get beheaded!

We played the Kentucky Derby the night before the race with Waylon Jennings and Crystal Gayle; that was pretty cool. My brothers and I were blessed to see a lot of places in our country and around the world because of our music and meet a lot of wonderful people; I'll always be thankful for that.

We were playing a show up in Lima, Ohio one night, we came off the stage, and our bus driver, Bass Man said, there's a guy asleep on the bus who says he's your Dad. My brothers and I have not seen nor spoken to my Dad since he and mom divorced. We approached my Dad with the intent of telling him to get off our tour bus, thankfully though things did not turn out that way. We had a very intense, direct, grown-up conversation. We mended our fences and that was that.

We worked a western medley of songs into our show, we brought our Dad on stage to sing it with us along with the Oak Ridge Boys' hit song, Elvira, the crowds loved it!

We're playing a New Year's Eve concert in Bowling Green, Kentucky at a place called The Runway. We were really kicking it that night; we do several encores after closing our show with the song, The American Trilogy. We went to our dressing room knowing we had just nailed it! Our road manager and lifelong friend, Beaver Hall comes in and says, "there's a guy out here, says he wants to talk to ya'll, he says it's very important. We told Beav, to bring him on in. Look, I know this next part is going to sound made up, but this is exactly how it went down....

A big man wearing gold chains around his neck, a big cigar and as confident as anyone I had ever met. He says, boys, my name is Clyde "Wee" Brown Jr.; ya'll can call me Wee. We did our introductions and out of the blue ole Wee says; I want to sign you boys!

We ask Mr. Brown exactly what do you want to sign us to do...? He says I own a coal company in Kentucky, I have plenty of money. I also like music but I can't sing or play a note. I own a music studio in Muhlenberg, KY, that is as nice or nicer than any studio in Nashville! I want you boys to be on my record label, CBO records (Clyde Brown Organization) and I want ya'll to be managed by my management company! We are sort of taken by surprise, this man means business!

We meet with Mr. Brown the next week, we cut a deal. Looking back on it now, this was not a good move for The Rangers. We should have just kept working the road with Mr. Peeples, and kept looking for that magical 3-minute song to come along! All the makings were here for what was needed to take the next step, but we lost control of direction, choice of songs. Just in general, it was not the right move.

Don't get me wrong, nothing against Mr. Brown; he was as nice of a man that you would ever want to meet. Mr.

Brown was not joking about his studio; it was very nice. To make a long story short, we signed with CBO records and Management Company in 1981. Mr. Brown had this guy who ran his Management Company, he was a super nice man, but he wasn't what we nor Mr. Brown needed to get the job done.

We stopped working the road and started listening to songs (mostly from Mr. Brown's publishing company). A song called "Crazy Woman," which was from Mr. Brown's publishing company, we figured out later that this song was really close to Mr. Brown. It was a decent song, but it wasn't what we needed to release as our first country single. We had better songs recorded that would have been a better choice. We released Crazy Woman in 1982; it went top 40 on Billboard's top 100 country hits. We had a full-page ad in Billboard magazine promoting the song and The Rangers, that was pretty awesome.

We followed that up with a new producer, Brian Fischer. Mr. Brown had hired him; he had previous success producing The Kendall's and their big hit song "Heavens just a sin away." The song we released was called "Roll with the Tide" it was originally about Alabama football, but it was nothing about Alabama football when he got through rewriting the lyrics. We felt hogtied, we were not on the road kicking ass and making money! We are on a salary that just got us by; we got very frustrated and called it quits in 1983.

We were all devastated that our dream didn't work out. My Dad went to Dothan, AL where he had his own radio show on a 100,000-watt station 95.5 WTVY. His show was number 1 in America for 23 years. He did this up until the time we lost my Dad to bone cancer in 2004. You should have seen the crowd at my Dad's funeral, you would have thought Elvis or Hank Sr had passed, sad day in Bama.

Bo went to work for Bob Frensley Ford in Nashville, TN selling cars, Big T went to work for an agency that booked Randy Travis, and I took a gig with The Temptations.

Otis Williams and I became friends; Otis is the co-founder and the last living (at the writing of this book) an original member of the famous Motown group. My first gig with the Temptations was in Memphis, TN at Mud Island. I toured with The Temptations and The Four Tops; The Temps and Tops were how it was billed. I have known a lot of singers in my day but none better than the lead singer with the Four Tops, Levi Stubbs, that man's voice was awesome! I never heard him sing an off-pitch note. The band leader was a man named Gil Askey; Gil was one of the nicest men I have ever met in my life. Gil and I had some great conversations over the many miles we traveled together. He always had the band and orchestra ready for the show!

Time goes by, Bo is still in the car business; he has moved up to management. Big T is still with the booking agency. I am now personal manager for a country music star, Terri Gibbs; her biggest hit was a song called "Somebody's Knocking." I got a pretty cool story to tell ya'll while I was with Terri Gibbs. We were out in San Jose, California playing at the Antelope Valley State Fair. We had just finished doing sound check and I had a few hours to kill before showtime. I took a walk around the fairgrounds; I came by one of those white tents you see set up at places like this. I heard someone playing the guitar. I pull the flap back, walk in and take a seat. No one else in there but the guy playing the guitar and me; man was he playing that guitar! He was practicing, I thought, man this guy is great! He finished what he was playing, looked up and said, hey man, how are you doing…? We started talking, an hour or so later I had just had a wonderful conversation with Stevie Ray Vaughn! It wasn't long after that, Stevie Ray was killed in an accident, music lost a great one that day!

My brothers and I have always been very close; we got together as much as we could. We all still felt the hurt. Big T tells us to never give up, we are going to make this happen, just wait and see!

Folks, my Brother Big T was awesome, he was the best closer I have ever known, if he ever got his foot in your door you were done, closed.

It is mid 80's; Big T calls me one night; Britt, I got us a deal to get The Rangers back together! It was like history repeating itself, I thought, here we go again. I listen and call Bo.

Big T and two guys (Ralph Savage and Eugene White) owned Sonrise Management Company from Columbus, GA. fly to Nashville, in their own personal jet, yep; I thought the same thing, who are these cats!

Bo and I pick them up at the airport; we go to the Stockyard restaurant in Nashville, and we listen to what they have to say. These guys tell us that money is no issue, they had put together one of the biggest cellular phone deals in history! They ask, "What it would take for them to own 25% of our group, for them to furnish the money to do what's necessary to get the Rangers back on track to become country music stars...? We told them this would not be a short-term deal; it would take time and effort on everyone's part and a lot of money to do what was needed. They didn't blink an eye and said; let's do it. Get us a proposal together, and send it to us.

We called our music attorney in Nashville, Brian Smith. We structured a deal and sent it down to Sonrise Management's headquarters in Columbus, GA, at 5:00 that afternoon we all agreed, we signed a five-year deal worth several million dollars! The money was to be paid to the Rangers every quarter for five years. We put together a plan of action and proceeded down the path of stardom!

Everything was going great; we were talking with a PR firm that was trying to sign us, The Pam Lewis Agency; the only other act she represented at the time was none other than Garth Brooks who was also trying to make it at the time. A funny story, Big T said to Pam one day in a meeting "Sugar, who would you rather have The Rangers or Garth Brooks" ....? It is quite funny now; but looking back on it at the time, Big T was 100% serious! I loved my brother; he was awesome.

We signed a producer to produce our session, Jerry Michaels. We acquired songs; we got the clearance to record them from the publishing companies. The songs were from great writers such as, Max D Barnes who wrote many hits including "Chiseled in Stone" a huge hit for Vern Gosdin. Paul Overstreet who also was a very well-known songwriter with many hits; Diggin up Bones by Randy Travis, and Same Ole Me by George Jones. Mike Reid is another great songwriter (Old Folks) hit for Ronnie Millsap, just to name a few. All these writers had given the Rangers some very good material. We finally had top-notch people working on our side!

We sign a Personal Manager, Sandy Ross. Sandy had just moved from New York to Nashville, he was looking for an act to manage. Sandy was a high-powered manager that had huge success with a group in New York called, Cameo. We had been in the studio, and cut 7 of the 12 songs we had acquired; out of those 7, everyone felt great about them all. We chose a Max D. Barnes song called "I am the Heart" to be our first release.

I had a friend in California named Dan Cunning who I had met when I was with Terri Gibbs. Dan called me one day and said, "Man Britt, I am hearing strong things about you and your brothers. Dan asked me if we would come to San Diego and do the Western Fair Buyers Associations showcase...? I told my friend, no problem, we would love to. We put that together and headed west. This was for all the fair buyers on the west coast, there are a lot of fairs and festivals on the west coast and we would be in front of them all!

A friend of mine who had played drums for Terri Gibbs (Bob Mummert) when I managed her later was playing with Roy Orbison when Roy passed away. I called Bob to see if we could get some of the musicians that played with Roy's band to play with the Rangers. We hired Roy Orbison's entire band, and headed to San Diego to play one of the biggest fair buyer's showcases in America.

We also play a show in Milledgeville, Ga at Sinclair Music Park, we open for John Anderson who was also in our booking agency. John's song "Swinging" had just gone gold. Let's just say we left that stage smoking! It was an hour after we left the stage that the show manager finally had to go into John's dressing room and tell John the crowd wasn't going to forget The Rangers tonight, that he had to go on and do his show. We had 40 shows booked with John Anderson. The next week, John told our agent that The Rangers couldn't open for him anymore. John said, I love the boys but they are too dynamic, I don't want to follow them! That's what the agent told us.

As I stated earlier, Otis Williams with The Temptations is my friend; we stayed in touch after I left the Temptations. Otis was very happy to hear about my brothers and me getting back together. Otis always told me the same thing Big T always said, "Britt, never quit." I was in the studio one day when I got a call, it was Otis. He said The Temps were playing at The Starwood Amphitheater outside of Nashville. He invited The Rangers to be his guest at their show. We were backstage; Otis surprised us when he invited The Rangers to join the Temptations on stage to sing with them! We were flattered and ready! My Girl never sounded better!

We did a show with Jerry Reed (The Alabama Wildman), it was the best show we had ever done, (not knowing this would be the last show we would ever do). That night was electric, it was by far the best show we had ever done. Folks, we didn't know it yet, but we went out with a huge bang!

The Rangers were back in the saddle again and riding hard! Things couldn't have been going any better! Then our world is shattered, once again....

One morning, I was at home getting ready to go into the studio to put the final touches on our release "I Am the Heart". I had the news on, the news lady says; Special Alert! The FBI is following a plane across the Atlantic Ocean, they believe that someone inside the plane has been shot! I thought to myself, man that sucks; little did I know, just how much.

The anchor lady continues her story; the name of the man inside the plane is believed to be Thomas Root! Mr. Root is an FCC attorney in Washington DC. My heart almost stopped; the CEO of Sonrise Management was Dr. Ralph Savage. I knew that Thomas Root was his attorney because we were in Dr. Savage's office one day while he was on the phone with him, he told Thomas Root he would get him some tickets to The Rangers concert when we were up that way.

Folks, I have never seen the wheels come off of something so quick! The FBI shut down all of Sonrise Management's accounts, including the one that funded our deal. Ralph Savage's and his partner Eugene White's personal accounts are all frozen. Imagine this, you are in business, and your money is cutoff cold without any prior warning, would that put you in a pickle...?

Well, I don't know what your answer is, but The Rangers were in big trouble! Not because we had anything to do with Sonrise Managements doings, heck I never knew what they did, but I never imagined it was crooked! Their troubles stemmed from trying to screw the FCC, how stupid can you be, trying to screw the #1 screwer of all time, the Federal Government!

We had a contract that was as solid as they came; we had made sure of that when we were structuring the deal. Even though it was an iron-clad deal, trying to collect it took time and money. It took several months to prepare our case, with attorney meters steadily running! It took all the money we had just for the preparation of a federal court case, it was a tough time for all of us.

Finally, we won a judgment for $2.8 million dollars in the Supreme Court of Tennessee. Eugene White was sentenced and sent to prison; Dr. Savage was sentenced to Federal Prison in North Carolina. The day he was reporting to start his time, he drove his car head-on into a tree somewhere in NC, it didn't kill him, so he pulled out his 9mm and finished the job. I'm truly sorry for those guys, but I tell you this, at the time I could have wrung both of their necks!

Look, regardless of what you might have heard about becoming a star, it isn't easy!

Do you remember the lowest point in your life...? This was a very tough time for me and my brothers and our families. We had obligations; we all were totally devastated. Not only were our lifelong dreams shattered again, the months of hard work we did, were gone!

It takes a lot of money to do what needs to be done, pay a band, lease tour buses, studio time and all the support people you need. At the time we just didn't have the will to start over again. Looking back on it now, we should have called Mr. Peeples and gone back out and worked the road until we could get things back on track, but we didn't, we just didn't have it in us.

My brothers and I go our separate ways once again, Bo went back into the car business, Big T went into the car business and I went back to building tanks with a company called, Chicago Bridge and Iron.

Several months later, Big T, Bo and I are talking; I'm telling them, man this tank work is a lot tougher than I remembered. They say to me, "Britt, why don't you get in the car business with us, it's great!" I asked them, doing what...? Selling cars! you would be a natural! I said, "Man, I can't sell cars, I don't even like car salesmen except for ya'll!" They closed me; I walked in a car lot, I learned from the best car men ever in my opinion, my brother, Big T, and Bo. Years later, a statement was made about my brothers and me; "Those Gilmore boys are great car men! It's like having your own game show host on your showroom floor"! Heck, they should have seen us hit the stage!

We have never looked back; I've been blessed in the automobile industry. I have worked for several public companies such as; Penske, Asbury, and Auto Nation. I have held positions ranging from a salesperson, sales manager, wholesale director, used car director, general sales manager, general manager and COO.

I have not thought about doing anything in music again, but I have a friend that almost tweaked my interest a few years back! I was General Manager for a Honda store in St Augustine, FL., my General Sales Manager was a guy that came to America playing with Carlos Santana's band, his name, Bob Houssami. Bob always tried to get me to sing, but I told him, brother, those days are over. Bob and his sweet wife Brooke are still our closest friends. Bob is also one of the best car men in our business.

My car business career is winding down now. Here's a story that happened that was quite shocking and quite frankly, stupid.

I was the COO of an automobile multi-store organization. I posted a comment on the EVIL sight of Facebook and it read, *"I can't believe any company would hire a THUG such as Colin Kaepernick to represent their company!"* Well, all hell broke loose because a racist black pastor stirred his racist followers to protest that post.

This was in September of 2018, back in March of 2018, I posted this post on the same EVIL Facebook "I can't believe these THUGS are doing what they are doing with a HOAX investigation of our President, Jim Comey, Peter Strzok and Robert Mueller are THUGS!

You know something funny; no one had an issue with that. I called three WHITE men THUGS, the same thing I called the "THUG" Colin Kaepernick, but the so-called racist pastor didn't have a problem with that. If by his actions, he associates the word THUG with black people, that goes to show you who the racist SOB in this story is.

Well, the little wimp of a CEO for this company calls me in his office and says, I'm going to have to let you go. I told him, "If this is the kind of man you are, I don't want anything to do with you or your company anyway."

Please, go back up a few pages, and read the piece I wrote on racism, you will see who the real racist was in this messed-up story.

I tried to retire after that fiasco in 2018 but I was bored sick! I took a year off, I went to Alabama in the fall/winter and hunted the entire season with my cousin Lightning, we had a great time. I played golf every day I could get to the course. I went fishing quite a bit. I'm going to tell you something when you get tired of fishing, hunting and playing golf, it's time to get your rump back to work!

My family and I move from Georgia to Tennessee. My wife Kristie and I live right outside of Nashville in Goodlettsville, TN.

Our son Luke is graduating soon from Middle Tennessee State University, Luke is a pilot. Luke is dating a very sweet young lady named Shelby Swaby. Our daughter Malia and her husband Erik live in Orlando, FL. They gave us three beautiful grandchildren; Norah, Braden and Asher! I never thought I could love someone like I do my kids, man was I wrong! I love my grandbabies!

Two of the toughest days of my life.

I was playing golf one day with a friend of mine named Tim Wilson. I got a call from my sister Tambo; Big T is gone. Man, that was a tough day.

The other toughest day was when Bo and Alisha's son Hunter passed away. Such a beautiful, precious little boy; I suppose God needed another little angel. That was heartbreaking for our family.

Dad, Mom, Hunter and Big T have gone on. Losing mom and Dad was really tough, but losing Big T and Hunter was different, almost an unbearable kind of hurt; I miss them all every day.

Big T, is survived by his wife Jodee, his childhood sweetheart, a daughter Shelby and a son Tanner and his wife Heidi, they have a son named Myles, Big T loved that little boy!

Bo and his wife Alisha live in Hendersonville, TN, they have a daughter, Hannah. Hannah and her husband Matthew Horne live in Tennessee as well.

My sister Tammy (Tambo), her husband Randy, their daughter Morgan and her boyfriend Tyler live in Tennessee.

My sister Kathy (Kat), and her husband Tim live in Tennessee, and their daughter Willy and her husband Gavin along with their daughters, Paisley and May also live in Tennessee.

Hey, you never know why things turn out the way they do. I know we were on the threshold of stardom in the music world. I know we were as good or better than some that did achieve that stardom.

Who knows, if things would have played out with our music, I might not have my wonderful wife, my beautiful kids, my precious grandkids; if that's the case; I have no complaints or regrets at all, I wouldn't trade them for all the stardom in the world!!

So, until we all meet again boys, in that Goldmine in the Sky, we will just have to wait and give it another shot!

Big T, Bo and Britt Gilmore.

Britt Gilmore.

Jerry Redd, Big C, Big T,
Britt and Bo Gilmore.

The Rangers

Britt Gilmore.

Britt and Kristie Gilmore.

Big T, Bo, Britt, and Big C.

The Rangers

Britt, Bo,
and Big T Gilmore.

The Rangers

Britt Gilmore

Bo, Britt and Big T

The Rangers

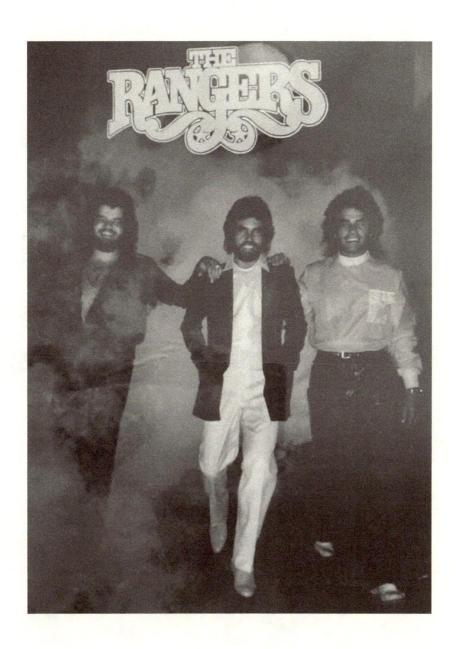

CPSIA information can be obtained
at www.ICGtesting.com
Printed in the USA
BVHW041448081022
648927BV00008BA/718